Building Brand

Mike Lingster

Aucta Books

CONTENTS

FOREWORD

I originally published this story in July 2000, and it was one of the more popular ones I ever wrote. A few months ago, a writer named Robclassact contacted me through deviantART and reminded me that the original version of the story ended with these words:

> Stay tuned for the Building Brand 2, due out about the same time George Lucas finishes Star Wars Episode 9.

And – he reasoned – that the release of *Star Wars: The Rise of Skywalker* fulfilled most of this condition, so there should be a sequel.

Now, when I wrote those words I didn't actually think there would ever be an Episode 9 – more than 25 years had passed between the release of *Return of the Jedi* and *The Phantom Menace* and I figured both George Lucas and I would be pushing up daisies before number 9 was ever completed – so I was leaving myself a big loophole in case I didn't want to write part two. And I found I did not want to write part two.

Helpfully, Robclassact offered to write part two, and I gave him my blessing. I've put a link to his story at the end of this one.

The story in this Kindle edition is cleaned up a little, and sporting a nifty new cover. I didn't try to bring it up to date. It remains set in 2000, before we had smartphones, social media, or Spotify. So,

trigger warning, the teens in this story actually experience conditions that include boredom, solitude, and not being able to immediately discover any fact they need.

Mike Lingster
Darien, Connecticut
March 2020

(I'm not actually in Darien but it seems a lot more like the kind of place you put in a book Foreward than the place where I am actually writing this.)

DAY ONE

Ryan could hardly contain his glee when he received his tube of Buck Studley's Hunk Cream in the mail. His parents were away on vacation for a week, and his sister wasn't home, so he was able to retrieve the package without having to answer any questions. He carried it upstairs, and opened the package on his bed.

The product came in a 12-oz tube, and was emblazoned with, "Buck Studley's Hunk Cream--Gain Inches, Gain Pounds!" A gigantically muscular arm was emblazoned across the label. Ryan eagerly flipped it over to read the other side:

Athletes of all ages have learned to appreciate the near-mystical power of Buck Studley's Hunk Cream# to aid in developing strength, mass, and healthy good looks. Whether to improve competitive performance or to attract members of the opposite sex, no product on the market today works like Buck Studley's Hunk Cream.

Directions: In a cool, dry place, drink 8 ounces of spring water and apply Hunk Cream to those parts of anatomy for which improved size and performance are desired. Remain immobile or nearly so for twenty minutes. Effects should begin within one hour, continuing for 12 to 15 hours. Apply every three days until desired effect is attained.

Important: Do not use in direct sunlight. Do not consume water or other fluids for at least two hours following application. Do not bathe for at least one hour after use. Do not use product on children or teens 18 years of age or under without the supervision of a physician. Under no circumstances should Hunk Cream# be used more than twice weekly. Do not engage in sexual activities for at least 12 hours after application. Hunk Cream may penetrate into the bloodstream and have residual effects throughout the body.

Caution: Failure to use this product in this manner may result in irregular or disappointing results, or in erratic, hypertrophic development. Under no circumstances should this product be used in a story written by a guy who gets a kick out of being beaten up by chicks. Under no circumstances should this product be used within 90 days of any other Buck Studley's or Buffy Bustout's product.

"Blah, blah, blah! This is going to be excellent!" Ryan exclaimed.

Ryan pulled down the shades, stripped off his clothes, drank a cup of water, dabbed about an ounce of the oily Hunk Cream into his right palm, and rubbed it all over his body, including his face, and especially (of course) including his penis. Then he sat down in a chair and starting reading comic books, intending to wait for a half-hour, just to be on the safe side.

About an hour later, Ryan was examining the most recent Adam Hughes Wonder Woman cover when he began to feel a strange sensation in his penis. Back in the days when Adam Hughes actually drew the art inside the comic books, as well as the covers, this sort of thing happened all the time. But given its scarcity, Ryan hadn't gotten an erection looking at new Adam Hughes art since about 1995, so he was a little surprised. Even the '96 Marvel Swimsuit Issue had been a disappointment. He began to do the math, figuring out the net margins on comic books, the extra copies of Wonder Woman likely to be sold as a result of an Adam Hughes cover, and was left stupefied as to how Adam Hughes could keep himself in Twinkies given such a ridiculously low level of productivity. But by then six or seven seconds had gone by, and as Masters and Johnson found, no red-blooded American male can go longer than that without thinking about his dick. It felt weird. His dick, that is.

Ryan peeled off his underpants (whoops, continuity error, the underpants were already off, don't you forget sometimes, too?), and looked down at his quasi-erect dumb-stick. Though only at half-staff, it seemed startlingly large! Like nearly everybody who ingests or applies some sort of magical growth formula, Ryan was astonished to find that it was actually-working!

"Whoa, it's bigger!" Ryan exclaimed, meaningfully.

He had always been a late bloomer, in fact until just two years ago his younger sister had been the taller of the two of them, and he was ecstatic that this cream would finally give him the chance to be the big guy. Ryan got up and posed in front of his mirror, flexing his muscles it was clear that he'd grown all over. He also felt incredibly thirsty, but the directions on the tube made it clear he wasn't to drink any water for at least another hour. In a narcissistic fury, Ryan spent the rest of the evening posing and checking out his new muscle and dick mass.

DAY TWO

When he hopped on the scale the next morning, Ryan found that he'd gained nearly ten pounds of muscle since applying Buck Studley's Hunk Cream the afternoon before, and a quick measure at the wall showed him to be taller. His muscles definitely seemed bigger, but just as impressively they seemed harder, and improbably strong. His face, which had also benefited from a generous application of Buck Studley's Hunk Cream, seemed more masculine and better looking, too. He was very satisfied -- he now stood 5'8" and weighed 135 pounds--and there were at least ten more applications in the tube! He could gain as much as 100 more pounds of hard, improbably strong muscle from this one tube, alone! He was quite impressed with the results, yadda yadda yadda, on to the girls.

Unlike most characters in stories like this, Ryan was very careful about where he left the tube of Buck Studley's Hunk Cream. As this story opens, Ryan had just finished his freshman year at Princeton (and we know how those self-impressed Princeton boys usually get a comeuppance in stories like this). As mentioned in the second sentence of this story, Ryan has a sister named Tara, and we know what usually happens in these stories when the male protagonist has a sister. Even worse, Tara has a really cute-but-undeveloped friend named "Barb Reas-Griltmig". Tara and Barb are both 18, they just finished their senior year of high school, and in just two months will be going off to college (never mind where, you perverts). Barb has a really big crush on Ryan, but because she's such a puny, scrawny, flat-chested, malnourished weakling of a cute girl, he's oblivious (isn't he just asking for this tube of magic gunk to fall into the wrong hands?). Still,

Ryan has also read stories like this one, and knows that the magic-growth-stuff-falling-into-the-wrong-hands storyline is the most overused and hackneyed plot-device since the Holodeck glitch. He doesn't do anything stupid with the tube, in fact he's got an old hiding place carved into the sheetrock of his closet, behind the molding. He puts the tube there before going to work at his summer job. He's sure his sister doesn't know about the hiding spot (but of course she does, DUH!!)

About an hour after Ryan left for work, Tara and her very cute (but puny) friend Barb went into his room, cut a beeline straight to the closet, and- borrowed a sweatshirt. (Whew, that was close!)

After work, Ryan headed up to his room and flexed some more. (He's sure impressed with himself, huh?)

A little while later, Ryan went downstairs to make dinner for himself, wearing no shirt, and encountered the lovely young nymphs, Tara and Barb.

"Hey, girls," Ryan said.

"Hey, how ya doing?" his sister responded, "How was work?"

"It was OK, same old."

Just then Barb piped up, "Have you been working out, Ryan? You look great!" Grabbing hold of one of his arms, she continued, "You feel really toned!"

"Well, yeah, I've been working out a little, here and there."

"Well, you look great," she added, adoringly.

"Thanks," he muttered, disinterestedly, eventually managing to separate his newly-buff arm from her cloying grasp, still oblivious to her interest, despite hints dropping faster than Bill Clinton's zipper.

All three headed into the den, to watch television and eat. When the news came on, Ryan was surprised to hear that all Buck Studley's Hunk Cream products had been recalled:

"Due to the possibility of dangerous, unspecified side-effects, the FDA tonight is recalling all Buck Studley's Hunk Cream products. Anyone who has purchased these products is asked to return them to the store from which they were purchased, or if they were mail-ordered, to call the number on the bottom of your screen."

Ryan was dumbstruck! Dangerous side-effects? What could they be?

Disconcerted, Ryan left the girls to go back to his room. He removed the tube of Hunk Cream from its hiding place behind the molding in the closet, and again examined the warnings for some kind of clue:

> Important: Do not use in direct sunlight. Do not consume water or other fluids for at least two hours following application. Do not bathe for at least one hour after use. Do not use product on children or teens 18 years of age or under without the supervision of a physician. Under no circumstances should Hunk Cream be used more than twice weekly. Do not engage in sexual activities for at least 12 hours after application. Hunk Cream may penetrate into the bloodstream and have residual effects throughout the body.
>
> Caution: Failure to use this product in this manner may result in irregular or disappointing results, or in erratic, hypertrophic development. Under no circumstances should this product be used in a story written by a guy who gets a kick out of being beaten up by chicks. Under no circumstances should this product be used within 90 days of any other Buck Studley's or Buffy Bustout's product.

Well, Ryan thought, the warnings seemed straightforward enough, and he was pretty sure The Author didn't get a kick out of men getting beaten up by women. He'd just be careful to make sure he followed the directions strictly. Return the cream? No way! This was his path to being a stud!

"Still," he thought, his mental syntax reflecting the razor-sharp analytical skills that had gotten him into Princeton, "it might be better to conceal the origin of the cream, in case mother were to find it."

Ryan contemplated this for a few seconds before deciding on a course. He went to the bathroom and dug out an old tube of tanning lotion, "Sun Bunny", from the previous summer. He emptied it out in the sink, and then washed out the tube a few times. Then, he poured the tube of Hunk Cream into the empty tanning lotion tube. Next, he took the actual Hunk Cream and left it in his hiding place in the closet. The empty tube he put in the trash in his garage.

Feeling his treasure to be safe, he retired early, so as to be better rested for work the next morning.

DAY THREE

About two hours after Ryan left for work, Barb Reas-Griltmig and another girl, Uva Zamnouptolous (her name in Greek means "painfully obvious anagram') showed up at the house (oddly, Barb's name in Norwegian means "less obvious anagram adapted from a story by Marknew"). Tara and Barb had been planning to spend the morning swimming in the pool and sunbathing, and Tara was just a little disappointed to see that Uva had come along. Uva was, well, astonishing in her beauty, and Tara felt completely inadequate around her, especially since Tara was a graduating senior, while Uva was just a sophomore. Uva was the new girl in school, having moved in next door to Barb only a few weeks earlier. Uva had hit the male population of the school like a class five tornado. Boys' hearts and egos were left strewn about the campus, waiting for someone in authority to declare a state of disaster.

While Barb had covered up for the trip to Tara's house, Uva was skimpily clad, wearing only a bikini and shorts, and carrying a liter bottle of Evian and a beach towel. Towering over Tara and Barb, Uva was 5'11" in height, with a long, curvy, athletic figure, and a big, firm, protruding pair of C-cup breasts. Tara guessed she weighed about 145 pounds. Tara, tall for her family, stood 5'6", nearly as tall as her brother, and while she had a somewhat curvy figure, her breasts were embarrassingly small. She weighed about 115. Barb was the smallest, downright puny at 5'2", with hardly a scrap of meat on her bones at all! Tara figured her for about 90 pounds. Barb was pale, and tended to be sickly as well, if she weren't an only child, the phrase "weak sister" would have Barb's picture next to it in the dictionary.

The girls watched TV for about a half hour, and then Uva suggested they go out back for a swim.

Uva was the first in, after removing the shorts she had on over her bikini bottoms, she showed off her athleticism with an incredible swan dive off the board. The other two girls entered less spectacularly. While Tara and Barb splashed around, Uva did a few precise laps. Tara was astonished to see the muscularity evident in Uva's arms and shoulders. When she was finished and came over to the other two, Tara asked her about it.

"Well, I work out a lot," Uva expained. "That's the only way to get muscles, unless you're born with them." To add emphasis, she flexed her right arm for the smaller girls, and a very solid, surprisingly large-looking array of muscles bloomed from the top and bottom of her upper arm. Her shoulder was also impressively thick and strong-looking.

"It looks like a guy's arm," Barb said.

Tara retorted, "You're just jealous because it's bigger than you thigh."

Uva shrugged. "I guess it IS as big as some guys', but not the guys I'm after," she said with a grin.

"It looks about as big as my brother's", Tara said, "maybe even a little bigger."

"Does he work out?" Uva asked.

"Oh, yeah!" Barb said, "He's getting pretty big! He's a hottie."

Tara rolled her eyes. "Yeah, he's got some weights in the basement."

"Oh, let's go look!" Uva said.

Before Tara could object, Uva had placed her hands flat on the edge of the pool, and in one strong motion had lifted herself poolside. Tara tried the same maneuver, but wound up flopping flat-chest first on the concrete. Barb went to the stairs to get out.

By the time they got downstairs, Uva was counting out "12" and racking Tara's brother's barbell.

"This is all the weight he uses?" Uva asked. "It's just 115 pounds. I bench 180 for five repetitions. Your brother's pretty weak for a guy."

This made Tara feel a little defensive. "I don't know, maybe that's just a warm-up. And you don't bench 180, that's bullshit." Growing up, she'd always been taller than her brother, despite the fact that he was a year older. He'd finally passed her in height about two years earlier. She knew how sensitive he was about being small. Plus she knew this amazon was full of crap about being that strong -- she wasn't nearly big enough to be THAT strong.

"Well, OK." Uva said, aware and embarrassed that she'd touched a nerve. "Let's go sunbathe."

Again the two smaller girls followed Uva upstairs.

Uva once again dived into the pool, but this time her top fell off as she plunged into the water. Uva swam some laps as if nothing had happened, and Tara felt herself staring at the new girl's big, sexy tits.

"Wow-" she said, unconsciously.

"You said it," Barb agreed.

Uva got out of the pool, and asked, "Hey, have you got any tanning lotion for my tits? I put on some waterproof stuff this morning, but not on my chest. I don't want to get burned."

Tara gaped, "Aren't you putting your top back on?"

"Why? It's just us girls."

"Uh, OK. Come to think of it, I haven't put any on yet, either," Tara said.

"Me neither," Barb agreed.

Tara ran upstairs and into the bathroom, looking for the tanning lotion. It wasn't there.

"Shit," she thought, "I just saw Ryan walking around the house with it yesterday. I hope he didn't take it to work."

Tara went into her brother's room and looked in all the usual places, but couldn't find it. Just on a lark, she checked the "secret" hiding place in his closet. She laughed -- she'd always gone through all his private stuff in there when they were younger. There'd be no reason for him to hide the lotion there, but, smiling, she thought there might be something else interesting in there.

As she pulled away the molding, the tube of tanning lotion fell out. She peeked inside, but there was nothing else there. Mission accomplished, she replaced the molding and went back downstairs with the tanning lotion.

She handed it to Uva, who squeezed a quarter-sized drop on her hand and rubbed it all over her naked tits. Uva then walked behind Barb and undid Barb's bikini top. Barb was clearly nervous about this, but when Uva bent over and rubbed her tits against Barb's skin-over-ribs chest. "Maybe some of it will rub off," Uva said, smiling.

"I-I hope so," Barb said.

As Barb began applying the tanning lotion all over her body, Tara removed her bikini top. She wasn't entirely flat, like Barb, but she still felt self-conscious in the presence of an busty girl like Uva.

In her turn, Tara also applied the lotion to all of her exposed flesh. She had burns from wearing a sleeveless top just a few days earlier, and so she rubbed extra all around her arms and shoulders. She also put extra on her chest, since the skin there was virgin-white.

Uva opened her Evian bottle and took a long drink. "Anybody?"

"Wait-I've got some inside," Tara said.

She came pack out with three more liter bottles of water.

All three girls drank from their bottles; quite a lot, it seemed to Tara, "How'd I get so thirsty?"

The girls were sitting out on the deck, taking in the sun, for about 20 minutes, before Barb started to make uncomfortable sounds.

"God, I feel like I'm burning all over! I'm going back in the pool!" With that, Barb got up and dove in. She stayed in for a few minutes, then got out and applied another layer of the lotion. She was really putting it on thick this time, Tara thought.

"Don't WASTE it, Barb! It's all I've got!"

"OK, OK, I'm done."

Barb chugged the rest of her bottle of water, and then opened the last remaining one, and chugged about half of that one.

"Barb, you're going to bloat up like a camel if you keep drinking like that!" Uva said.

"I'm just so thirsty! Hot and thirsty! I feel really weird," Barb said back.

"I feel pretty hot, too. I had this sunburn all over my arms and shoulders, and it feels like it's getting worse. I'm burning all over, but it's especially bad there. It's so bad it hurts!" Tara said.

"Mmmm-yeah, my chest is burning a little, too. How old is this tanning lotion?" Uva asked.

"Last summer, I think," Tara smirked.

"Well, we've been out here about 40 minutes-maybe we should go back inside?" Uva suggested.

"Yeah, OK," Tara said, and got up and put her top on.

Uva put hers on as well, but Barb didn't budge.

"I thought you felt weird," Tara said to Barb, "aren't you coming in?"

"It's a good kind of weird-" Barb said, "I feel really, I don't know, just good."

"All right, we're going inside, though," Tara said.

Tara and Uva went inside, while Barb stayed out in the sun. The two girls stayed inside for a little while, chatting about school and boys, but after a bit Uva stood up and said, "Well, I'm outta here. I'll see you."

"Aren't you going to wait for Barb to drive you home?"

"Nah'I'll walk. A little exercise never hurt. And it's only about a mile."

"OK, see you," Tara said.

About ten minutes after Uva swaggered out, Barb came back into the house, groaning.

"Uva was right, I'm bloating all over," she moaned.

"Well, what do you want me to do? Do you want to sit down?" Tara asked.

"No-urgh-.burp-.I'm going to head home, and go to sleep."

Barb struggled wearily with her clothes, a sweatshirt and a pair of shorts, but finally got them on, and then put her sneakers on.

As Barb walked out the front door, Tara could hear sloshing sounds coming from the backyard.

Tara went to the backdoor, and saw that the faucet was running. "

MIKE LINGSTER

"Jeez-how much water did she drink?"

UVA'S PROFILE GETS MORE-PROLIFIC

Uva had only reached the top of Tara's block when she started to feel strange. Her breath was a little raspy, and she felt slightly weak. She kept walking, but began to feel increasingly uncomfortable. After a few minutes, the discomfort passed, and she picked up her pace. Her breathing felt tremendously relaxed, and she straightened up even more than was her habit, though she'd always valued good posture. She was a little surprised by the sensations of her breasts moving inside the bikini top, maybe it was because she was using such good posture, but the top felt very tight.

A carful of boys drove by at just that moment, and yelled some lewd comments at her. Uva had gotten used to this sort of behavior, though the boys seemed even more enthusiastic than usual. She pretended to be offended, but inhaled deeply and stuck out her chest, simultaneously swelling with pride and maximizing the visual effect of her bosom.

"Ouch!" she cried out loud, "That's tight!"

She relaxed her chest, but her breasts seemed to be protruding unusually far out from the rest of the body. She moved her hands up to the bottoms of her breasts quickly, and hefted them up so they'd settle back down into the bikini top, but she was surprised to find no "give". Her breasts were completely filling the cups of the bikini! She stopped walking and looked down at her cleavage.

Uva watched as stretch wrinkles appeared in the fabric of her bikini top, as though she were thrusting her tits out. But she was standing completely still. She could feel it happening -- her breasts were growing! No wonder those boys were so excited, she had to be fronting a pair of double-D's to the world by now!

"How could this be happening?" she said out loud, "I stopped using Buffy Bustout's Spectacularly Stacked, Strong N' Sexy (motto:

"Knock the boys out, one way or another!") last week! What's happening to me?"

The strings on her bikini were really cutting into her sides, now.

Uva ran off the street, behind a hedgerow. Her gigantic breasts bounced exuberantly up and down as she went. Once under cover, Uva untied the strings of her bikini, took a deep breath, and then she retied them, leaving as much free room as possible. She headed home as fast as she could, her mammoth mammaries jiggling and jostling back and forth, up and down as she went. Her center of gravity was completely off, but the strength and agility she'd gained from Buffy Bustout's Spectacularly Stacked, Strong N' Sexy seemed to be greater than before, and she was able to keep her good posture intact, even as she rushed home.

When Uva finally reached the driveway of her house, she noticed that Barb's car was already in the driveway next door. Then she noticed that the guy next door on the other side was gaping open-mouthed at her chest.

"Didn't your mother teach you any manners?" she yelled at him.

"Didn't yours teach you any modesty?" he yelled back.

She had to admit he had a point.

Uva didn't feel as if her breasts were still growing when she reached home, but the bikini top was packed tight. She stood in front of a full-length mirror in her mother's room, and took off her clothes. She simply couldn't believe how big her breasts had become, but they didn't sit like the gigantic tits she'd seen on the Internet--they were round and full, and firm. No saggy, baggy elephant, she. When Uva faced away from the mirror, raised her arms in the air and looked back over her shoulder, she could see several inches of her breasts protruding to the sides of her lats in the mirror. And her lats seemed different, too. In fact, now that she noticed, her muscularity seemed to have increased somewhat, too.

She grabbed a tape measure from her mother's sewing kit. It was difficult to do alone, but she managed to lift her breasts up in order to get the tape under them. The measure read 36 inches'which was about an inch more than it had been the last time she'd measured, the week before. Then she managed the tape across the fullest portion of her gigantic, abnormally firm breasts. It came out as 43 inches!

"Good God," she thought, "That's a-41, no, a 42F!!" Yikes!"

She flexed her right arm and played the tape around the widest part of her upper arm-15 inches! Again, an increase of about an inch.

Measuring her waist, she found no increase-still 25 inches, and her waist was still 34 inches, "Damn Greek ass!" she thought. She stood up against the wall and marked it, then measured down to the floor'still 71 inches. Then she got on the scale, and found that she had gained almost twenty pounds!

"Where did it all go? I weigh almost 170 pounds! Yikes! I better keep that part to myself."

Uva felt outstandingly strong -- she had stopped taking Buffy Bustout's Spectacularly Stacked, Strong N' Sexy gel caps about 10 days earlier, because she was afraid she becoming too tall and too muscular. She wouldn't have minded growing one extra cup size, though, and somehow, today, she'd gained THREE, without getting too much bigger everywhere else. She felt so much stronger, way out of proportion to the extra muscle she'd packed on!

Buffy went down to the basement, where her weight set was located. She grabbed two 25-pound plates and slipped one on each side, and then replaced the collars. The bar was now 230 pounds. Uva Zamnouptolous lowered her body onto the bench, and slowly lifted the bar off the rack, and lowered it to her chest -- well, as far to her chest as it could go -- and then raised it. She did it five more times before she racked it.

"Wow!" She stood up and flexed, in yet another full-length mirror (notice a pattern here?).

"I am a big-titted super-strong amazon girl!" she screamed, a cry she'd screamed before, but now she really meant it.

"But how did this happen?" she wondered. Uva went up to her room and found a pair of panties and jeans, and put them on. The panties went on fine, but the jeans felt unusually tight over her newly-muscularized thighs and calves. The tightness felt satisfying, it reminded her how strong she had become. Realizing that she no longer owned a brassiere that had cups that could contain a quarter of her massive bosom, she went straight to her shirt drawer. She looked around until she found something appropriate.

"Ooooh-my Gap ribbed T-shirt! That should look spectacular!" She pulled it on, feeling delight as it stretched, stretched, and stretched some more over the gargantuan mounds of her breasts. The ribbing was showing incredible separations, far beyond the designer's intentions and the boundaries of good taste. It exaggerated the outrageous dimensions of her bust beyond all credulity. As she struggled in vain to pull it down to her waist, she noticed another attractive aspect of the shirt'the ribbing stretched very attractively across her newly swollen, muscular arms and shoulders. She turned sideways in the full-length mirror on the back of her door (keeping count?), and gasped at how outrageously sexy she looked. She sucked in her abdomen and stuck out her chest, and did a double-biceps flex in the mirror'"Fantastic," she said, smiling.

Uva went back to her dresser and dug through her underwear drawer'mostly now filled with Goodwill fodder'until she found the half-empty jar of Buffy Bustout's Spectacularly Stacked, Strong N' Sexy. There was a picture of a pretty blonde girl -- the usual cheerleader type, at first glance -- in a pose that was a cross between cheesecake and bodybuilder pose. A skinny guy, not quite as tall as the blonde, was standing next to her, with his mouth open in shock. It wasn't clear whether he was ogling the girl's bulging muscles, which were significantly larger than Uva's, or her bulging breasts, which were somewhat smaller. It was clear, however, that the bodaciously developed blonde was ignoring her scrawny admirer. The label read, "Buffy Bustout's Spectacularly Stacked, Strong N' Sexy -- Knock the boys out, one way or another!" Uva turned the jar over and read the directions:

> Women of all ages have learned to appreciate the near-mystical power of Buffy Bustout's Spectacularly Stacked, Strong N' Sexy to aid in developing strength, beauty and a curvaceous figure. Whether to achieve physical strength that will make you the equal or the superior of the boys, or to drive them crazy with improved curves, physical attractiveness and vigorous, athletic good health, no product on the market today works like Buffy Bustout's Spectacularly Stacked, Strong N' Sexy.
>
> Directions: In a cool, dry place, take two caplets of Spectacularly Stacked, Strong N' Sexy with 8 ounces of spring water. Remain immobile or nearly so for twenty minutes. Effects should begin within one hour, continuing for 12 to 15 hours. Take two caplets every three days until desired effect is attained.
>
> Important: Stay away from direct sunlight for at least 1 hour after ingesting gel caps. Do not consume water or other fluids for at least two hours following ingestion. Do not bathe for at least one hour after use. Do not use product on children or teens 18 years of age or under without the supervision of a physician. Under no circumstances should Spectacularly Stacked, Strong N' Sexy be used more than twice weekly. Do not engage in sexual activities for at least 24 hours after application. Spectacularly Stacked, Strong N' Sexy may affect some parts of the body more than others.
>
> Caution: Failure to use this product in this manner may result in irregular or disappointing results, or in erratic, hypertrophic development. Under no circumstances should this product be used in a story written by a guy who gets a kick out of being beaten up by chicks. Under no circumstances should this product be used

within 90 days of any other Buck Studley's or Buffy Bustout's product.

She had followed the directions religiously! It shouldn't be causing these sorts of erratic results, she thought. It worked out all right in this case, but looking down at her breasts, which covered the entire front of her body from just above the midriff to her collar-bone, and two or three inches out on either side, and knew that getting bigger wasn't really practical. No man would ever make eye-contact with her again.

BARB BLOATS, THEN BULGES, THEN BURSTS OUT OF HER CLOTHES

Barb didn't feel very good. She could feel her belly sloshing around as she walked out to her car, and there was a weird tingly sensation all over her body. Even her head felt weird -- her face, her fingers, everywhere. And she was still thirsty!

She made a wrong turn headed home, and wound up going the long way around, but it only added a minute or two to her trip time.

Barb staggered into her house -- she couldn't believe how bloated she felt! Her clothes even felt tight! All over! And she felt so heavy!

Walking up the stairs to her bedroom, Barb suddenly felt a little better. In just a few seconds, she felt a whole lot better, although she still felt tingly all over. Something about her leg caught her eye -- it looked wrong. She looked down at it and was surprised to see some muscle there. Actually, there was a fair amount of muscle there, a lot more than she'd ever seen there before! What muscle was it? The quadriceps, she thought, that was the muscle that had gotten so big in her leg. And when she looked, it was both legs! And all the muscles in them! Suddenly, she had muscular legs.

"How could that happen?" she wondered, "God, my shorts are TIGHT!"

Barb sat down on her bed, and noticed for the first time that she had grown breasts, too! She couldn't see them clearly, but there were definite bumps protruding from her sweatshirt. And when she felt them, they seemed pretty big.

First things first, she had to get the shorts off, they were really starting to hurt! She tried to pull them down, though, and there wasn't any way to get the waistband over her hips!

Suddenly, Barb heard, and felt, her shorts ripping, the waistband had given way. She reached down and grabbed the remnants of the shorts, and somehow managed to tear them right off her body. Still wearing her bikini, she could feel a strain against the top.

When Barb reached up above and behind her head, she heard the sleeves begin to rip on her sweatshirt, just as she pulled the shirt up and over her head. It didn't want to come free of her breasts, or of her arms, but she finally worked it loose.

What she saw astonished her.

In the mirror, a very muscular and fairly busty young woman was looking back at her, and Barb was shocked to realize it was herself. The bikini top, one of those Spandex numbers with a band around the back and over the shoulders, was overflowing with titflesh in the front, and stretched across the cordlike trapezius and lattissimus dorsi muscles that had blossomed from her slender frame.

Still, though, she was thirsty. Barb went into the bathroom and began shoveling handfuls of water into her mouth -- pint after pint. The thirst was overpowering. She stepped on the scale after she'd drank her fill, and was astonished to see the needle come to rest at 122 pounds.

"I weighed 87 pounds this morning! How-how on earth did I gain 35 pounds in a couple of hours? This is impossible!"

Just then, Barb felt a strange tingly feeling wash over her body.

Looking in the mirror, she watched as her whole body began to change again. Her face had always been very cute, but now it seemed more adult -- maybe even beautiful?

Her breasts swelled against the top. She watched it happen! Her breasts pushed outward and upward, spilling out the front of her bikini. The stitching began to go -- she could hear the zipper rip apart, and her brand-spanking-new tits sprung fully free from their prior restraint. Barb cupped her breasts and lifted them up

-- they were huge! At least a C-cup, she figured. And the arms that hefted them up'she couldn't believe how muscular they'd grown!

Barb flexed a double biceps pose in the mirror'and there was no doubt about it, she now had the physique of a bodybuilder. And as she watched, her arms grew thicker, stronger. It felt incredible!

"Look at these muscles!! I am so strrrrrong!!"

Further, Barb noticed that she could see her abdominal muscles in the bathroom mirror'but she'd never been tall enough to see below her chest in that mirror.

She ran downstairs to the garage of her house, where her father had drawn a measure on the wall to measure her height when she was little. Balancing a ruler on top of her head with her right hand, and kissing her baseball-sized bicep as her arm held it there, she made an etching on the wall where the ruler met it. After turning to look at it, Barb gasped again -- five-foot-five!

"I've grown three inches and put on God knows how much muscle in the last hour and a half! What the Hell is going on? It seems to happen when I drink water..."

Barb went to the kitchen and grabbed a Tupperware pitcher from the cabinet. It was a half-gallon container; she filled it to the brim, and went upstairs. She began slurping the water down and almost immediately began to feel her muscles and breasts swelling again. Her forearms were growing before her eyes, thick cords of muscle pushing a spider web of veins to the surface. She watched her big, perfect breasts increase in size as she drank the water.

"Stronger," she said, in between breaths and slurps of water. Finally, exhausted, she finished the water and crawled into bed.

At some later point, her mother knocked on the door to the room, and asked her if she was coming down for dinner.

Barb drifted out of sleep and said that no, she didn't feel so good and wanted to stay in bed.

Then she fell back to sleep.

TARA OUTMUSCLES HER BROTHER

Tara found herself wondering about what it was like to be strong and athletic, like Uva. What a body that girl had! Muscle in all the right places, tits in all the right other places -- Uva really had it all going on. And so unselfconscious! Tara wondered if she could ever be so shameless and unembarrassed about her body as Uva.

"Maybe if I had something to show off, I'd want to show it off," she thought.

On a lark, she went down to the basement and contemplated her brother's weight set. Uva had handled those big clanky metal things with admirable strength and poise, but to Tara they were completely alien. Well, not completely -- on the soccer team they'd worked out with weights on rainy days sometimes -- but she had never gotten used to them.

For a second the image of Barb, scrawny, weak little Barb, trying to work out with weights entered her mind. She laughed out loud.

"She'd probably kill herself with one of those barbells."

Giving in to temptation, Tara sat herself down on the bench and lay back on it. She put her hands on the barbell, as far apart as she could manage, and slowly lifted it off its mountings. She held it in the air for about a half second-and then slowly lowered it to her chest.

"115 pounds-this isn't so bad, I can do this."

As she lowered it further, though, Tara realized that the weight was far too much. It was all she could do to keep from dropping it onto her chest. Once it was pressed against her chest, she couldn't get it back up. Tara tried as hard as she could, but couldn't manage it. Worse, she couldn't manage to slide it off to one side. She tried to roll it off her ribcage, but it hurt more once it reached her abdomen, and it took all her strength to roll it back up to her chest.

She was feeling very queasy, and having trouble breathing due to the weight on her chest. She wasn't sure she could hold out until Ryan got home to help her, in about an hour, but even if she did, she'd be so embarrassed to need that kind of help!

Starting to cry, Tara felt absolutely awful. Her chest hurt, her sunburn hurt, she felt nauseous and tingly -- she just hadn't had a good day, and now it was worse. But after a few minutes, she felt a little better. Her breathing was somewhat easier, and the weight didn't feel quite so oppressive.

Marshalling her strength, Tara inhaled deeply and tried with all her might to lift the barbell off her chest. And with great effort, she could feel it moving!

"Go-.go go go!!!" she cried.

She felt nearly exhausted, but the higher it got, the less effort it seemed to require. Finally, she was able to rack it. Tara was breathing heavily -- the effort had been enormous.

With new appreciation for Uva's strength, Tara sat up and took deep breaths until she felt like herself again.

That's when she noticed her arms. She could see a vein protruding from each bicep muscle, and aside from that, both arms just looked-bigger. Her arms seemed thicker than they had been before.

"That's probably just from the strain of getting that thing off my chest," she concluded, and got up to head back upstairs.

As she was going, she remembered that Ryan kept a scale in the corner of the basement, and went over to weigh herself.

"One-twenty-two? But I was only 115 the other day!" Tara said, aloud.

She looked down at her belly, but there was hardly any fat there at all, less than she was used to. Running her hands up her body, Tara noticed that her breasts seemed -- could they be bigger? Could her breasts have grown?

"And what about my arms?" she asked.

There was an old bathroom mirror mounted behind the weight bench, and Tara went over to it and flexed her arms. Distinguishable biceps rose from her arms.

"I never had those before, I'm sure of it!"

She placed her left hand on her right harm, and felt a sinewy strength that was new.

With a mischievous look back at the bench, Tara again lay back on it and put her hands on the bar. Again she lowered it to her chest, but this time she felt much more control. Next she raised it, with far less effort than had been required before. She racked it, then waited a minute, and then lowered it again.

Tara found herself now able to do four repetitions with the bar. There was a preacher curl pad behind the bar rack, and Tara next took advantage of this. Her brother had two dumbbells sitting beneath it, each with 25 pounds. Grabbing one, she clumsily rested her upper arm on the inclined pad, the way she'd seen her brother do it. It was heavy, no doubt, but she found herself able to do 15 with each arm!

"I feel terrific!" she said, surprised.

She stood up and looked in the mirror again and there was no doubt: she was bigger. In fact, she thought she was closing in on Uva in terms of muscle size!

Tara found two ten-pound and two-five pound plates on the floor. She put 15 additional pounds on the barbell, and then lay down to press it.

When she first tried to lower the bar, it was a little like the first time -- it banged into her chest with more force than she would like -- but she felt a sponginess in the impact. Lifting her head, she was able to see the contour of actual breast flesh inside her top.

At first struggling to raise it, Tara felt a sudden wave of strength come over her, and easily thrust the bar skyward. Holding her arms erect, she was able to see impressive muscular development all along her arms, and in her shoulders, too.

"This is so cool!" she shouted.

She began doing reps with the bar, and unlike before, each one got easier rather than harder. At 20, she quit, her arms more muscular than she ever imagined they could be.

And when she got up, it was apparent that it wasn't just her upper body that had changed. Her legs, always a little on the skinny side, were now resplendently full, with elegant shape added by pounds of new muscle. Her ass, too, now had a curve to it that she knew would drive boys crazy.

She grabbed her breasts next and was astonished to find that she'd gone from almost totally flat-chested to something in the range of a B or C cup.

The only things out of proportion on her new body'the body of a fit, curvy woman, were Tara's arms and shoulders. They had become unusually muscular for a girl. She was pretty sure they were bigger than Uva's arms, now. She was dead certain they were bigger than her brother's. She walked over to the scale and stepped on it.

"145 pounds! Good God! I've gained thirty pounds in the last-hour? Shit, Ryan will be home soon-I can't let him see me like-.and his hiding spot!"

Tara ran upstairs and grabbed the suntan lotion from off of the patio, and then ran into Ryan's room and replaced it in his hiding spot in the closet. Then she ran into her room and grabbed the sweatshirt she'd borrowed the day before, and threw it on. Then she grabbed a pair of pajama bottoms and pulled them on, before heading back downstairs. She flopped down on the couch just as Ryan came in the front door.

"Hey Tara," he said.

"Hey," she replied.

Ryan went directly into the kitchen and opened the refrigerator.

"Hey, you want anything?"

"What've we got?"

"Lots of stuff," he said.

Tara got up and walked into the kitchen'Ryan was faced away from her, looking into the fridge.

She came up behind him, and suddenly realized she was looking down on his head.

"AH!" she cried, suddenly aware that she'd gotten taller -- significantly taller -- just as she'd grown really strong and somewhat busty.

Ryan started to turn around, "What?" he asked.

Tara was quick, she immediately sat down in one of the chairs around the kitchen table.

"Nothing, just saw a... stepped on... I just got a little dizzy flash." She lied.

"Errr... OK. Do you want me to get you something?" he asked.

"Could you get me a glass of water?"

"Sure," he replied.

While Ryan turned his back on her to fetch the water, Tara sprinted back into the den and flopped down on the couch.

A minute later, Ryan came in with the water, and sat down along-side her on the couch.

Tara sipped the water eagerly while they watched TV.

After a few minutes, Tara began to rub one of her arms, feeling the new muscularity through the fabric.

"Hey!" Ryan exclaimed, "Isn't that one of my sweatshirts?"

"Uh-yeah. I borrowed it yesterday."

"You should really ask."

"I know, sorry," she responded.

Ryan continued to look at her as she shifted her gaze back to the TV.

After a minute of being stared at, she looked at him and said, "What?"

"You look different," he said.

"How?"

"I'm not sure-have you gained some weight?"

"Maybe."

Tara took another gulp from her glass, and then felt a weird, but familiar, tingling spread through her body.

Because she was wearing clothing all over her body, this time she could feel it happening. Tara felt the soft fabric of the sweatshirt sliding along her skin as her breasts grew. She could also feel the cuffs on the sleeves and pants sliding up her wrists and ankles as she grew taller, and the folds in the armpits and elbows shift as her arms, already so muscular, began to bulge with new power!

Her chest was already bigger around than her brothers, and she was suddenly aware that he was staring at it. From her perspective, as well, she suggested, from his, it looked as if balloons were inflating under the sweatshirt.

"What-the?" he said, finally.

She could feel the sweatshirt tightening around her chest, but the sleeves were also getting tight, as her arms continued to swell with unwanted muscle!

Ryan stood up and grabbed her by the wrist, and tried to pull Tara to her feet. He couldn't budge her.

So he reached further in and put his hands around her upper arms, as if to wrench her forward, but then an astonished look came over his face.

"What happened to your arms? They're bigger than -- well, they're really big for a girl!"

She stood up, finally, and he watched her as she rose and rose some more to her feet. She was at least three inches taller than her brother, now.

"You've been using my Hunk Cream! Damnit! That's not right!"

He stepped closer to her, in anger, but was surprised to find her breasts protruding well out in front of the rest of her.

"Well, I hope you're happy'you've turned yourself into a circus freak! Maybe now you can get a job as one of those WCW... CHOKE!!!"

Tara had lifted him up under the armpits and pushed him up against the wall, holding him aloft.

"Look, LITTLE brother," she began, "all that I've used of yours today was your weight set -- and by the by I am WAY stronger than you now -- your sweatshirt, and some suntan lotion that my friends and I used, that I found in your not-so-secret hiding place. Nothing else!"

As Ryan stared at her, dumbstruck, Tara felt another wave of strength wash over her.

"Oh, no! Not again!" she cried.

"What?" Ryan asked.

He soon had his answer. Ryan felt her grip tighten painfully on his rib cage, and saw his sister's breasts swell to new levels of voluptuousness. He heard a tearing sound, and watched astonished as the shoulders and sleeves of his sweatshirt began to tear as Tara's arms became even stronger.

When the growth had passed, she tossed him onto the couch, and then stormed upstairs to her room.

Ryan sat downstairs for a few minutes, and then went upstairs to his room, to check his hiding spot. The Hunk Cream was back where we had left it, but only about one-quarter of the tube remained.

"How did she get so big, so fast?" he wondered, "She must have grown almost six inches today! When I used it, I only grew about a half inch."

Ryan went downstairs and made himself some dinner. Then he went back to his room and applied, as per the instructions, another dose of the Hunk Cream. He went to bed after that.

DAY FOUR

Ryan woke up early for work, but decided before he was even out of bed that he would call in sick today, and try to figure out how his sister had gotten such outstanding results from one day's treatment of Buck Studley's Hunk Cream.

He was disappointed to see that he hadn't gotten anything like those kind of results from his previous night's application of the product. Still, he'd gained about an inch in height, and gained a whole 15 pounds, so he was now about 5'9, 150 pounds.

"Tara's at least 5'11", and God only knows how heavy. And her arms! Man! Mine look like twigs next to hers."

Ryan considered that there were only about two, maybe three, doses left of the Hunk Cream. If he could get the same results as last night, he might, maybe, wind up as tall as Tara, and about as muscular, assuming she hadn't grown anymore during the night.

He really had trouble accepting the irony of his situation.

Ryan went down to the basement to pump some iron, and was surprised to find himself struggling with the bar. Then he realized that Tara had moved the weight up to 145, which wasn't so bad. He ran through his usual upper-body workout, curls, lats, delts, abs, and was fairly satisfied to see improvement of 20-30% in all of his maximums. But the knowledge that his little sister could rip his arms off without even trying took some of the euphoria out of it.

When he went back upstairs, Tara was sitting at the kitchen table, eating breakfast. She had ripped the remnants of the sleeves off his t-shirt, and was wearing it. Her arms and breasts were massive, but the rest of her body, though still muscular, was closer to normal human proportions.

"I hope you don't mind me wearing this," she said, "it's the only thing that fits anymore."

"No sweat," he said. "You don't look like you grew anymore last night."

"I don't think I did."

"Well, that's good..." he suggested.

"Yeah," she said rolling her eyes, "we wouldn't Ryan to look even smaller next to his sister, the freak."

"Well -- I didn't mean it that way."

"Hey," she said, "you look bigger this morning."

"Yeah, I took another dose last night'I've had two, now."

"Really? How did I get so big from just one?"

"I was hoping you could tell me-there's not a whole lot left in the tube."

"Can't you get more?" she asked.

"No, it's been recalled. "Unidentified side effects," he responded.

Tara nodded, "I guess we found out what they are."

"Yeah."

Just then the phone rang.

Tara answered it, "Hello?"

"Oh, hi Barb. Hey did .. it did? Yeah, me too. Why don't you come over? You'd better bring Uva, too, after all, she was there. OK, see you in a few minutes."

Ryan looked at his sister. "Barb and who?"

"Uva Zamnouptolous," Tara said, "Oh, you'll like her-gorgeous, tall, athletic and with big tits."

"And Barb said she got bigger, too? How much?"

"She didn't say," Tara explained, "But she was a five-foot-two inch 90-pound-weakling. Maybe she's normal sized, now."

A few minutes later the doorbell rang. Ryan ran to get it and peeked out the little window. All he could see was some dark fabric -- probably just some Jehovah's Witness coming around in a suit.

He opened the door and found himself eyeballing the biggest tits he'd ever seen.

Looking up, and up, and up, he finally found himself looking into the face of a breathtakingly beautiful woman, who had to be at least six-foot-five. She looked a little familiar, but he was sure he'd remember such incredibly beauty. He stuttered for a second, and then noticed that her arms, which were bare, were easily twice as muscular as his sister's. Her legs were like curvy tree trunks. They looked like they could crush cars. Looking back up into that achingly beautiful face, framed by golden tresses of hair, he finally gathered his composure and asked, "Are you ... Uva?"

"No, silly! It's me, Barb! Barb Reas-Griltmig!"

"B-b-barb!?"

Barb Reas-Griltmig was wearing a Michigan sweatshirt, cut off at the shoulders, like his sister. She had also cut off the collar, and cut a six-inch slit down the middle of the chest, right between the "H" and the "I". The sweatshirt only made it down to the bottom of her breasts. Below that he could see incredibly well-developed abdominal muscles, and then her incredibly powerful-looking legs.

Barb stepped through the door, and Ryan had to step to the side to let her through -- she was gigantic. She reached over and tousled his hair, and then stopped and said, "Are those the same muscles you had yesterday?"

"Actually, they're bigger," he said.

She smiled seductively, "Mine, too! I guess everything's relative -- you seemed so big, strong and manly yesterday, but now you look like such a little cutie."

He wasn't quite sure how to take that, when he heard another voice.

"Hi, I'm Uva."

Looking around, he was confronted with a girl who was of much more normal proportions than either his sister or Barb, except for her chest, which was absolutely gigantic.

"Let me guess," he began.

"Gold star, smartass," she responded, "Yes, I only put the cream on my tits. But I did get a lot stronger last night, and I was practically doing one-arm curls with you barbell even before that, so don't think you can push me around."

"Whoa-no problem."

From the kitchen, he heard, "Barb? Little Barb? What the hell happened to you?"

"Same thing as you two, just a whole lot more of it, I'd say. I went out into the garage this morning to measure myself. I am six-feet-fucking-five!! And just for laughs I crawled under my dad's Jeep Wrangler and bench-pressed it."

"Bullshit!" Uva said.

"Totally not bullshit! I don't know what was in that suntan lotion, but it turned me into the strongest, sexiest girl on the fucking planet. I lifted a car off the ground, just like one of those hydraulic presses at the gas station!"

Ryan was shocked that he felt attracted to her, but she was dead right that she was the sexiest creature he'd ever seen. He couldn't take his eyes off of her, and his penis, bigger than ever, was straining against his pants.

Barb made eye-contact with him. "See? Look at your brother -- he wants me so bad he can't stand it."

"Barb," Tara said, "you're acting a little... aggressive, don't you think?"

"Duh! I'm the strongest person in the world, Tara! What's anybody going to do about it?"

She walked over to Ryan and lifted him up, one-handed, by his shorts.

"Come on Romeo, I'm the world's hottest virgin, and you're going to teach me some things."

Barb threw Ryan down on the king-size in the master bedroom, straddled him and ripped his clothes off.

"Wait," he gasped, "the directions on the Hunk Cream say not to have sex within twelve hours of use' and I used it about ten hours ago."

"Well, in two hours I'm not going to be a virgin anymore, one way or another. So take your pick, I can have any guy now. Besides, I didn't follow any stupid directions, and look what happened to me!"

With that, Barb did a double-bicep pose. "Would you believe they're 22 inches? I measured this morning."

With that, Ryan began to grab her gigantic breasts under the sweatshirt.

Barb pulled it off, over her head, and then slipped out of her shorts. She then grabbed Ryan's shorts and tore them off with one pull.

His hands were all over her -- her muscles, her huge breasts -- and she was so gorgeous!

She lowered herself onto him, and began rubbing back and forth. He managed to slip his penis into her as she came down, and then her bucking began to became more aggressive. He was incredibly stimulated by her knockout figure and incredible beauty, and began to struggle vigorously beneath her. Several times he tried to flip her over to get on top, but each time she smiled condescendingly and pressed him back down into the mattress with one hand.

Ryan could feel a fire building in his loins, and knew he was about to have a massive orgasm. He tried to change the rhythm of their gyrations to match his need to slow down and maximize the experience, but Barb's strength was such that he had no more power than a nine-volt dildo. Her lovemaking to him had the feeling of contempt about it, or at least resentment. Normally that would bother him, but goddamn it, was she hot!

He began to come, but he was astonished at the length and volume of the experience. He felt like gallons of cum were passing through his penis'he could feel himself slipping down in the sheets as it progressed, as if he were being swallowed by the bed.

When it finally ended, Barb said, "What the hell happened to you?"

"Orgasm," he panted, feeling unusually severe post-coital weakness.

"Yeah, yeah," she continued, "I meant, what the hell happened to your body? You're like, half the size you were before."

To drive the point home, she lifted up one of his arms and held it in front of his face. He was shocked! It was emaciated, and completely bereft of any shape or definition!

"Ha ha!" she laughed, "You're not much bigger or stronger than I used to be! You're going to be taking that Buck Studley stuff for a while, huh? I guess I was wrong, you SHOULD have stuck to the directions."

"But-I'm almost all out of it," he said, numb with shock.

"Buy more!"

"I-I-can't. It's been recalled from the market."

"Oh. Well. I guess I'm sorry, I thought you could get your size back the easy way. Y'know, being small's not the worst thing in the world. And if you work out, maybe..." Barb trailed off.

She seemed momentarily confused.

"Ohhhh-." She moaned, "I think I know where all your size went."

Before his very eyes, the amazon giantess began to grow even taller, and more muscular. Her breasts swelled even further, and her impossibly muscular arms clearly began to bulge with new muscle. She seemed as if she would explode with her new power.

For his part, Ryan used his new puniness and Barb's lengthened thighs to slip out from beneath her. The whole room seemed larger to him now, and he realized that he'd lost a lot of height, too, in addition to muscle mass. He pulled on his shorts, which luckily featured a drawstring, and ran as fast as he could down the stairs.

He ran face first into a gigantic pair of breasts, which turned out to be Uva's.

He quickly turned to the right, and saw his sister's big tits, also at eye level.

"What the hell happened to you?" Uva and Tara asked in unison.

"I shrunk when I had sex with Barb, and she got bigger," he

shrugged, still in shock. He couldn't really see the girls' faces'their tits were more or less at the same level of his head, and significantly larger. They effectively obstructed his view of anything above tit-level on his sister and her friend.

"She's BIGGER?" Uva asked, slackjawed.

"How much bigger?" his sister asked.

Just them the whole house shook -- Barb was getting out of bed.

BOOM... BOOM... BOOOM... the windows rattled with each step. She slowly made her way down the stairs -- everyone was astonished at how utterly huge she'd become.

As she reached the second to bottom step, her head crashed into the sheetrock in the ceiling.

"Whoops", she said, "Looks like I'm about as tall as your ceiling. What is it, seven feet?"

"Yeah," Ryan said, sighing. The three girls were standing fairly close together, and he was in the middle. It made him feel very child-like, and somewhat depressed. He still couldn't see faces -- with Barb he couldn't even see the fronts of her tits, just the bottoms.

"Well," Barb boomed, "I'm going out on the deck to sunbathe."

Once she was gone, Ryan let loose.

"What the hell am I going to do? I can't go back to work or school like this! I'm, like, a 90 pound weakling!"

With that, his sister flexed her massive arms and said, "Yeah, these will be real guy magnets at school. You know how guys like girls who can curl Buicks. I'm going to die a ridiculously muscular virgin."

"Relax!" Uva said. "Those Buck Studley and Buffy Bustout products can solve both your problems. There are growth formulas," she said looking at Ryan, "and reduction formulas for Tara and Barb. The reduction formulas are marketed under the name Wanda Willowy's Slim and Shapely. Everything will be all right."

"Shows what you know," Ryan said, his voice grating like the pipsqueak he'd become, "those products have been recalled. We'll never get them."

"A-hem," Uva continued, "that might be a problem, if my Uncle Bucky and Aunt Buffy weren't the manufacturers. How did you think I got this body in the first place? Come on, I'll go with you to their house. Me first, though, a half day with these tits is more than enough. I want to get back down to a bra size in the first half of the alphabet."

"Yeah," Tara said, "but how will we get Barb to take any reduction formula? She's hooked on being a giantess. It's like her whole personality has changed, and not for the better."

"We'll cross that bridge when we come to it, I guess," Uva said, "Let's go see my uncle."

△△△

The End

ACKNOWLEDGEMENT

If you want to read more about the adventures of Uva, Barb, Tara, and poor shrunken Ryan, a different writer named Robclassact has published a sequel at his site.